The Balancing Girl

by Berniece Rabe
pictures by Lillian Hoban

A PUFFIN UNICORN

Text copyright © 1981 by Berniece Rabe
Illustrations copyright © 1981 by Lillian Hoban

All rights reserved.

Unicorn is a registered trademark of Dutton Children's Books

Library of Congress number 80-22100
ISBN 0-14-054876-9

Published in the United States by
Dutton Children's Books,
a division of Penguin Books USA Inc.
375 Hudson Street
New York, New York 10014

Editor: Ann Durell   Designer: Susan Lu
Printed in U.S.A.
First Unicorn Edition 1988   COBE
10   9   8   7   6   5

To Rochelle Rabe

Margaret was very good at balancing. She could balance a book on her head. She could glide along in her wheelchair as nice as you please, and the book would not fall off.

She could even balance herself and hop with her crutches.

At school she collected the Magic Markers and balanced them in neat rows on the shelf. Ms. Joliet said, "You have a very steady hand, Margaret."

Tommy said, "Anybody can do that. Who couldn't do that?"

Right while Tommy watched, Margaret balanced twenty blocks in a tower.

"That's simple," he said.

"Then you do it," said Margaret.

But Tommy wouldn't try. He just said, "I still say it's simple."

Margaret planned and planned. She wanted to do something very special that Tommy could not call simple.

She got out of her wheelchair. She pushed some regular chairs together just so. And she made a private corner for her work.

It took a long time and great care, but at last she finished it. She finished a fine castle made of six cylinder spires, with a cone balanced gently on top of each.

Jannie and William clapped for the castle.

But Tommy said, "That's simple. I build castles like that at home all the time."

Margaret would have shouted at him if Ms. Joliet had not said, "Time for recess."

When they came back into the room after recess, Margaret's castle was knocked down. Flattened out!

Tommy was the first person to shout, "I don't know who did it!"

Ms. Joliet had to leave the room just then. It gave Margaret a chance to say, "Tommy, you had better never knock down anything I balance again, or YOU'LL BE SORRY!"

Tommy was just starting to yell back when Ms. Joliet came back with Ms. Howard, the principal. Margaret hoped Ms. Howard was going to give Tommy a good scolding for knocking down her castle.

Ms. Howard said, "We are going to hold a school carnival to raise money for more gym equipment. And we need ideas for carnival booths."

Quickly Tommy raised his hand. "At my big brother's school carnival, he and my daddy ran a fishpond. People paid to fish for presents. My daddy and I could run a fishpond booth."

Everyone clapped for Tommy's idea. Even Margaret.

"Good," said Ms. Howard. "Are there any other suggestions?"

At last William said, "I guess I'll be a clown."

Tommy said, "Clowns don't make money."

Margaret raised her hand. "I saw a clown once who sold balloons." Margaret liked William.

"That's the kind of clown I am," said William. "A balloon-selling clown."

No more ideas came, so Ms. Howard left.

At the end of the day, Ms. Joliet said, "Now will each of you put on your thinking caps and see if you can come up with a good carnival idea by tomorrow?"

Well, it was no trouble at all for Margaret to balance a thinking cap on her head. She thought and thought. Even while she slept, maybe.

The next morning she whispered something in Ms. Joliet's ear.

Again Margaret made a private corner. In the farthest part of the corner, she started setting dominoes on end. Very gently, very carefully she placed each domino just a small distance away from the last one. She had to be so very, very careful, for if even one little finger touched a domino and made it fall, then one by one they would all come toppling down.

She used up all the dominoes that belonged to Ms. Joliet's room. Ms. Joliet borrowed more from the second grade.

Margaret made fancy curves and snaky S's. Ms. Joliet borrowed dominoes from the third grade.

Margaret made little stairs and let the dominoes march up and down them. Ms. Joliet said it was time for recess.

Tommy yelled dibs on the great big ball. He gave it two big bounces. It would have gone right into Margaret's domino corner if William hadn't jumped and caught it.

"Outside today!" said Ms. Joliet.

Ms. Joliet was careful to lock the room when they left.

The next day Ms. Joliet borrowed more dominoes. Just about everybody stood and watched while Margaret continued to make a whole city full of highways and byways. They watched even during snack time.

Margaret never saw who dropped a cookie right in the middle of the long S chain.

She moaned. "I can't reach back to get it out. One slip and my whole city is gone!"

"I'll get it for you," said Tommy.

Ms. Joliet caught his arm just in time and held him back. "I will do it, Tommy," she said.

The whole class held their breath. Even Ms. Joliet held her breath as she reached over and got the cookie.

The next day Margaret finished placing the last domino. Everyone begged and begged to be the one to push down the first domino. Even Tommy begged to be the one.

Margaret announced, "The name of the one to do that will be pulled out of a hat. AND you will have to pay to get your name in that hat."

Ms. Joliet said, "The name will be drawn from the hat the last night of the school carnival."

Everyone clapped. Margaret was very happy and
pleased. She was so happy she forgot to watch where
her foot was. As she started to move out of the
corner, her toe hit the end domino.

Click, click, click, click, click, click! Six
dominoes fell down. But then they stopped.

They had come to a corner.

Oh, she had left too big a space.

Thank goodness.

Gently, very, very, very gently, she put the six dominoes back upright. This time she made the space at the corner just perfect.

"O-h-h-h-h-h wow!" yelled the class.

"Don't scare me like that again!" said Ms. Joliet. "Class, you are all appointed guards of this corner from now until the end of the carnival."

That was one really great school carnival.
Margaret visited every booth. And she
bought three balloons from William.
She tied the balloons to her chair.

When she went to get a present from the fishpond, Tommy was standing out in the hall. He was watching people go up to his booth.

Margaret asked, "Why aren't you working, Tommy?"

Tommy didn't tell her to shut up. He said, "My daddy has too much help. I guess he's got a hundred people helping him. Even my big brother."

"Oh," said Margaret. She fished in the pond anyway. She got a rubber spider.

She didn't have a chance to show it to Tommy, for a loudspeaker announced, "Time for the Grand Finale, folks. Let's move along to the first grade room and see who gets to push down that first domino."

There was lots of pushing and shoving, but Ms. Howard was good at waiting. She waited until everyone was gathered as close as possible to Margaret's corner. Then she let the oldest person in the room draw the name from the hat. It was Jannie's great-grandmother.

Jannie's great-grandmother put on her glasses. Then she read,

Tommy pushed to the front of the crowd. He
stepped inside the domino corner. He stood there
for a long minute, looking at Margaret.

"Well, push," said Margaret.

Tommy pushed harder than was needed, but still it went beautifully. *Click, click, click,* a thousand times *click,* the dominoes took their turns falling. It seemed like it took hours for them all to fall.

A big cheer went up!

And Tommy looked right at Margaret and yelled, "There! I knocked down something that you balanced, and I'm not sorry."

"I'm not sorry either,"
called back Margaret.
"I made a hundred and
one dollars and thirty cents,
the most money in this carnival."

"Hurray for the Balancing Girl," someone shouted.

And Margaret was sure she heard Tommy join in with the big cheer that went up.